For Griffin and Holly,
because everything I do is for you.

And Errol, for all the love
and for introducing us to the East Coast.

Thank you, also, to my friends the Reid family,
and to Paul Kinsman for his help and guidance.
—L.S.

Illustrations and illustration notes copyright © 2022 by Lauren Soloy

22 23 24 25 26 5 4 3 2 1

Greystone Kids / Greystone Books Ltd.
greystonebooks.com

Cataloguing data available from Library and Archives Canada
ISBN 978-1-77164-833-2 (cloth)
ISBN 978-1-77164-834-9 (epub)

Editing by Kallie George
Copy editing by Linda Pruessen
Proofreading by Doeun Rivendell
Jacket and text design by Sara Gillingham Studio
Expert review by Paul Kinsman
Disability awareness review by Karen Autio

Printed and bound in Singapore on FSC® certified paper at COS Printers Pte Ltd.
The FSC® label means that materials used for the product have been responsibly sourced.

The illustrations in this book were created digitally.

Greystone Books gratefully acknowledges the Musqueam, Squamish, and Tsleil-Waututh peoples on whose land our Vancouver head office is located.

Greystone Books thanks the Canada Council for the Arts, the British Columbia Arts Council, the Province of British Columbia through the Book Publishing Tax Credit, and the Government of Canada for supporting our publishing activities.

Lauren Soloy

THE BELOVED FOLK SONG

I's the B'y

GREYSTONE KIDS

GREYSTONE BOOKS · VANCOUVER/BERKELEY/LONDON

Sods and rinds to cover your flake,

Cake and tea for supper,

Hip yer partner, Sally Tibbo!
Hip yer partner, Sally Brown!

Fogo, Twillingate, Moreton's Harbour,

All around the circle!

I don't want your maggoty fish,

They're no good for winter.

I could buy as good as that
Down in Bonavista.

Hip yer partner, Sally Tibbo!
Hip yer partner, Sally Brown!
Fogo, Twillingate, Moreton's Harbour,

I took Liza to a dance,

As fast as she could travel!

Hip yer partner,
Sally Brown!

Fogo, Twillingate, Moreton's Harbour,

All around the circle!

I's the B'y

Very rhythmically

1. I's the b'y that builds the boat, And I's the b'y that sails her!
2. Sods and rinds to cov-er your flake, Cake and tea for sup - per,
3. I don't want your mag-got-y fish, They're no good for win - ter.
4. I took Li - za to a dance, As fast as she could tra - vel!

1. I's the b'y that catch-es the fish And takes 'em home to Li - za.
2. Cod-fish in the spring o' the year Fried in mag-got-y but - ter.
3. I could buy as good as that Down in Bon - a - vis - ta.
4. And every step she did take Was up to her knees in gra - vel.

Chorus

Hip yer part-ner, Sal - ly Tibbo! Hip yer part-ner, Sal - ly Brown!

Fo - go, Twil-lin-gate, More-ton's Har-bour, All a-round the cir - cle!

Notes from the Illustrator

Hello!

"I's the B'y" is a traditional folk song from Newfoundland, Canada, written over 100 years ago. It was popularized by Gerald S. Doyle's book *Old-Time Songs and Poetry of Newfoundland*, and has been recorded by numerous musicians. It's my treat to illustrate it, to celebrate the way music brings us together, and to share some of the unique character and beauty of this place. In making these illustrations, I was inspired by the people, places, and traditions of Newfoundland. Here's an explanation of some of what you'll find in these pages:

I's the b'y that builds the boat: Newfoundland dialect is full of wonderful phrases. "I's the b'y" (pronounced "eyes the by") means "I'm the boy," but "b'y" is now considered gender neutral. This spread was inspired by the Isles Wooden Boat Museum in Twillingate.

And I's the b'y that sails her!: The characters in this spread are rowing a traditional Newfoundland boat design called a "dory." Icebergs are seen in the water at certain times of the year.

I's the b'y that catches the fish and takes 'em home to Liza: "Liza" here would likely have handled and processed the fish. Also, laundry really does dry in the winter!

Sods and rinds to cover your flake: A flake is a platform to spread out and dry your fish for preserving. "Sods and rinds" seem to refer to the clumps of grass and bark that were used for this purpose.

Cake and tea for supper: Cake and tea usually means a simple meal. This illustration shows a popular "cold plate" meal in Newfoundland—cold cuts, tomatoes, and different kinds of potato salad. (The bright pink one is beet and potato salad, and it's delicious!)

maggoty, maggoty, ♫ ♫ maggoty, maggoty!

Codfish in the spring o' the year, fried in maggoty butter: "Maggoty butter" here doesn't necessarily mean the butter has maggots, or fly larvae, in it. It refers to how the butter might have been older in the spring, when supplies were running low. This illustration shows a collection of fishing huts and stages, where the catch would be brought to be prepared or stored.

I don't want your maggoty fish, they're no good for winter. I could buy as good as that down in Bonavista: "Maggoty fish" here means poor-quality fish. (The word "maggoty" is also an excellent word to produce a rhythm with—try it! Sing "maggoty, maggoty, maggoty, maggoty. . ." and see if you don't find yourself bobbing

your head to the beat.) Bonavista is a coastal fishing town. Nearby, the town of Elliston is a fabulous place to view puffins.

I took Liza to a dance: This illustration shows two iconic Newfoundland things—berry picking and root cellars (essentially a hole in the ground with a door). Many houses still have these old-fashioned refrigerators!

As fast as she could travel: Newfoundland ponies, shown here, are an endangered breed of pony.

And every step she did take was up to her knees in gravel: Perhaps this line refers to the gravel roads of the day—it's open to interpretation.
I couldn't resist a MerB'y here in this image. MerB'ys were started by the Newfoundland and Labrador Beard and Moustache Club, whose members dressed as mermaids and sold calendars for charity. The inclusive group's only membership requirement is that you "appreciate facial hair."

The chorus of "I's the B'y" is all about the dance! Folk dancing comes in many forms, including the circle dance. The beautiful thing about a circle dance is that it is simple, flexible, and inclusive. In a circle dance, we are all equal. Fogo, Twillingate, and Moreton's Harbour are located in the same coastal area of Newfoundland.
It's one of my favourite places in the world.

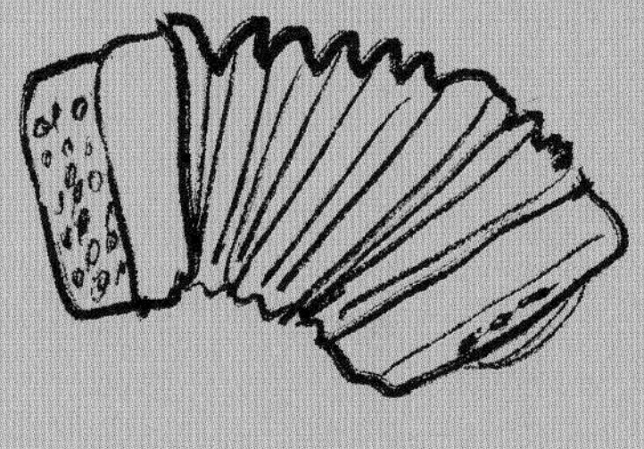

With love, Lauren